Natalie Quintart & Philippe Goossens

PIRATE
John-Wolf

Clavis

NEW YORK

John-Wolf is often called a *weakling*.

When the teacher asks him to come to the blackboard, he feels weak.

When someone runs off with his snack, he feels weak.

When a fly lands on his nose, he feels weak.

When a girl looks into his eyes, he feels weak.

But when John-Wolf
is alone in his room….
He sings about the heroic deeds
of pirates like Blackbeard,
Calico Jack and Captain Hook.
Then, John-Wolf becomes *as hard as* **nails.**

One night, John-Wolf the Weakling
is suddenly *kidnapped* from his room!
The pirates take him to the open sea.

John-Wolf ends up on the pirate ship
NO MERCY

On deck, Tomcat, Wooden Leg,
One-Eye, Hook, Bear, Beak
and Captain Drake glare at him angrily.

"So, why aren't you singing about the heroic deeds
of the great Captain Drake?"
When the pirate looks into his eyes,
John-Wolf feels as weak
as a lump of lukewarm butter.

"I um… k-know the stories a-about da-dangerous pi-pi… rates,
but I h-have ne-ever heard about cap-cap… tain… Drake."
What?! *Sniveling brat*, sing or I'll throw you overboard,
as my name is Captain Drake!"
"For-for… give me, cap-cap… tain, b-but m-maybe you could
t-tell me some more about your he-heroic deeds first?"

"Hey Captain," One-Eye laughs, "there's a ship with a bunch of poor devils aboard. Shall we go after them?"

"Look, my boy!"
Captain Drake yells.
"A galleon! Board her
and NO MERCY!"

When a pirate
howls in his ear,
John-Wolf feels as weak
as porridge.

John-Wolf hides away in the ship's hold,
but Captain Drake finds him
in no time.

When the pirate drags him along to the bridge,
John-Wolf feels as weak
as a slimy snail.

"Take a good look at
this spectacle, so you can
sing about my heroic deeds later.
Do you see how **strong** and *quick*
my pirates are?"

When the fight
on deck breaks out,
John-Wolf feels as weak
as a custard bun with strawberries.

Suddenly, the captain of the galleon grabs ahold of John-Wolf.
"Look, little squirt, do you see how long my saber is?"
Luckily, Captain Drake was keeping an eye on the boy
who will sing about his heroic deeds later.

"Hey, you sly dog, *let go of the little guy*
or I will make you eat that saber,
as my name is Captain Drake!"
When two pirates pull on his arms,
John-Wolf feels as weak
as a lump of toothpaste.

The dreadful fight is over.
John-Wolf cringes when he hears
the thunderous voice of Captain Drake:
"Well, what are you waiting for?

Sing about **my** heroic deeds!
I saved your life, boy!"

All the pirates on **No Mercy** gather
around him. They are waiting for his song.
John-Wolf takes a deep breath. Now he is going
to sing about Captain Drake's heroic deeds.
Now John-Wolf the Weakling is going to feel
as hard as nails. But… nothing comes out of his mouth!

"Dagnabit!" the captain roars.
"What's the matter? Are you making fun of us?"

John-Wolf takes his little notebook
and writes with tr_embl_ing fingers:
I am sorry, my dear pirates,
but I have lost my voice!

Impatiently, the pirates wait for their captain
to read John-Wolf's words.
"Hm, hmm," Captain Drake says while clearing his throat.
Then, he reads aloud:

*"Oh, Captain Drake, strongest, bravest and handsomest
of all pirates, before I can write my song,
I first need to endure*
the **four Trials of the SKULL.**"

John-Wolf cannot believe his ears.
Captain Drake doesn't know how to read!
He is just *making things up*!

When Bear pushes him into a cannon,
John-Wolf feels as weak
as the meat
in a sausage.

When Wooden Leg suspends him
from the crow's-nest,
John-Wolf feels as weak
as a sail without wind.

When Beak tickles his feet
with a seagull's feather,
John-Wolf feels as weak
as bird droppings.

When One-Eye pushes him onto the gangplank,
above a sea filled with sharks,
John-Wolf feels as weak
as fish food.

"Captain, let's divide the stolen loot!"
Tomcat suddenly yells. "We'll get to your song later."
"Yes, the loot!" Bear repeats.
"The treasure is ours!" the pirates shout in unison.

Together, they sit down around the loot and the barrels of rum.
They drink away and stuff themselves with food,
while they sing songs and brag about their fights.
John-Wolf looks from one pirate to the other in amazement.
It seems they have forgotten all about him!

John-Wolf starts singing. First very quietly, but then louder and louder:

"Look, the pirates and their loot,
after lots of rum and food,
they're as weak as rotten fruit!"

Captain Drake, the worst one, opens one eye.
"Hey, John-Wolf, have you **finally started singing**?
Start again, will you? I didn't hear you all that well."

"Look, the pirates and their loot,
after lots of rum and food,
they're as weak as rotten fruit.
After all, they seem to
have forgotten to give me some too!"

Furious, Captain Drake pulls out his saber.
But John-Wolf feels as hard as nails
and is singing at the top of his voice now.

"They only read things in reverse,
and just their very favorite verse.
Look, the pirates and their loot,
after lots of rum and food,
they're as weak as rotten fruit.
And then, they all start to snore,
those pirates are just a bore."

"Darnit, you little rascal, I should cut out your tongue.
But you are a brave little brat and I like that.
All right, I will call you John-Wolf the Pirate Singer!
If you want, you can stay here with us,
but maybe you can change
a *couple of things* in your song."

And that's why **John-Wolf the Pirate Singer** now sails the seven seas. He's Captain Drake's best friend.

On land, nobody calls
him John-Wolf the Weakling any more.
John-Wolf the Pirate Singer
is what everyone says with awe.
And in schoolyards and playgrounds
you can sometimes hear this song:

"When the teacher calls him to the blackboard,
he walks like he is stepping aboard.
When someone runs off with his snack,
he smiles and quickly gets it back.
When a fly tries to land on his nose,
he doesn't even let it come close.
When a girl looks into his eyes,
he smiles like he's got a big surprise.
John-Wolf Pirate Singer, that's what they call him."

For Bénédicte, Vincent, Espoir and Arthur,
four merry pirates
N.Q.

First published in Belgium and Holland by Clavis Uitgeverij, Hasselt – Amsterdam, 2015
Copyright © 2015, Clavis Uitgeverij

English translation from the Dutch by Clavis Publishing Inc. New York
Copyright © 2017 for the English language edition: Clavis Publishing Inc. New York

Visit us on the web at www.clavisbooks.com

Pirate John-Wolf written by Natalie Quintart and illustrated by Philippe Goossens
Original title: *Piraat Jan-Wolf*
Translated from the Dutch by Clavis Publishing

ISBN 978-1-60537-330-0

This book was printed in March 2017 at Publikum d.o.o., Slavka Rodica 6, Belgrade, Serbia

First Edition
10 9 8 7 6 5 4 3 2 1